Announcement :
Hector,
rhinoceros from Java,
is not responsible
for debts
incurred
by Jules and Francis,
shoes.

Shhh

WORDS AND PICTURES BY PATRICK COURATIN

A Harlin Quist Book

Published by Harlin Quist, Incorporated / Library of Congress Catalog Card: 74-6875 / ISBN Trade: 8252-0116-0 / ISBN Library: 8252-0117-9 / Text and art copyright © by Patrick Couratin and Harlin Quist / All rights reserved / Color separations by Vontobel Druck AG / Printed in Switzerland by Vontobel Druck AG / Design by Patrick Co

For some unknown reason,
Gladys,
an apple rotten to the core,
wanted to communicate
with Jules and Francis,
shoes,
born of a Javanese father
and a Hungarian mother,
each usually occupied by a foot,
each foot usually covered by a stocking.
But, instead,
Gladys communicated
with Janice,
a cow,
daughter of a steak,
future steak.

For some unknown reason,
Janice,
a cow,
daughter of a steak,
future steak,
wanted to communicate
with Hector,
rhinoceros from Java,
who was blessed
with a practical physical defect,
and who was in no way related
to Jules and Francis,
shoes.
But, instead,
Janice communicated
with an anonymous hand.

Hector,
rhinoceros from Java,
who was blessed
with a practical physical defect,
and who was in no way related
to Jules and Francis,
shoes,
wanted to communicate
with Mr. Milhous,
a rich man,
who was rich
for reasons still unknown.
But, instead,
Hector communicated
with Gladys,
an apple rotten to the core.

Mr. Milhous,
a rich man
who was not very well-bred,
wanted to make contact
with Janice
for an eventual communication.
But,
for reasons unknown to this day,
Mr. Milhous,
a rich man
who was not very well-bred,
and who was rich
for reasons still unknown,
communicated
with Stanislas,
a duck of strange origin.

Stanislas,
a duck of strange origin,
wanted to communicate
with a duck
who wanted to communicate
with a duck
who had communicated
with a man.
But,
with the aid of an anonymous hand,
Stanislas
communicated
with Janice,
cow,
daughter of a steak,
future steak.

Dwayne,
a duck whose origins
are unknown to this day,
wanted to communicate
with a duck
who had communicated
with a man.
But, instead,
Dwayne communicated
with a duck
who wanted to communicate
with a duck
who wanted to communicate
with a duck
who had communicated
with a man.

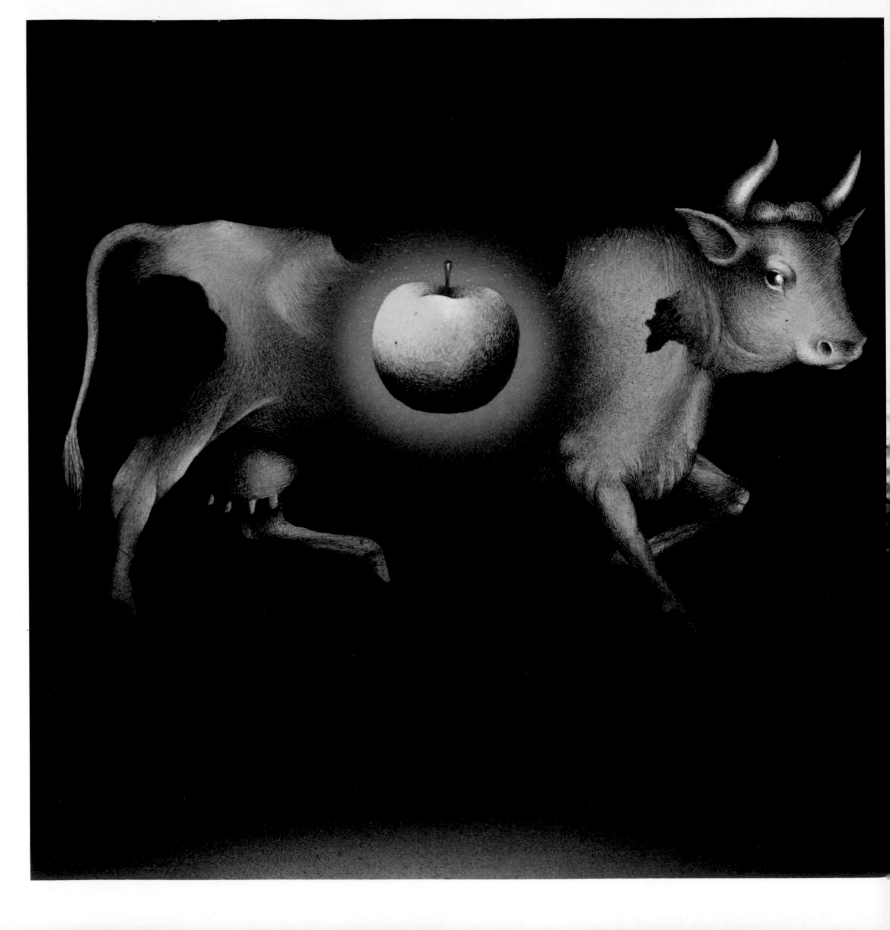

For some unknown reason,
Gladys,
an apple rotten to the core,
was about to communicate
with Jules and Francis,
shoes,
born of a Javanese father
and a Hungarian mother,
each usually occupied by a foot,
each foot usually covered by a stocking.
But,
in fact,
Gladys was none other
than Janice,
cow,
who had always been rotten to the core.

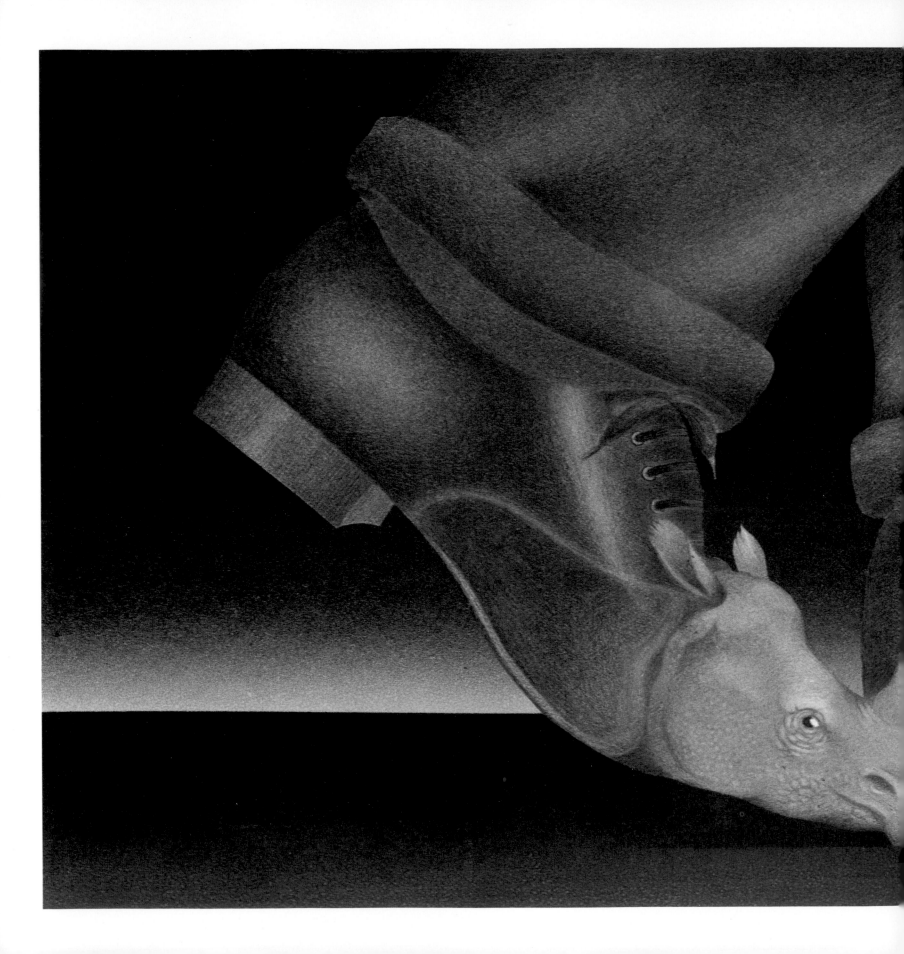

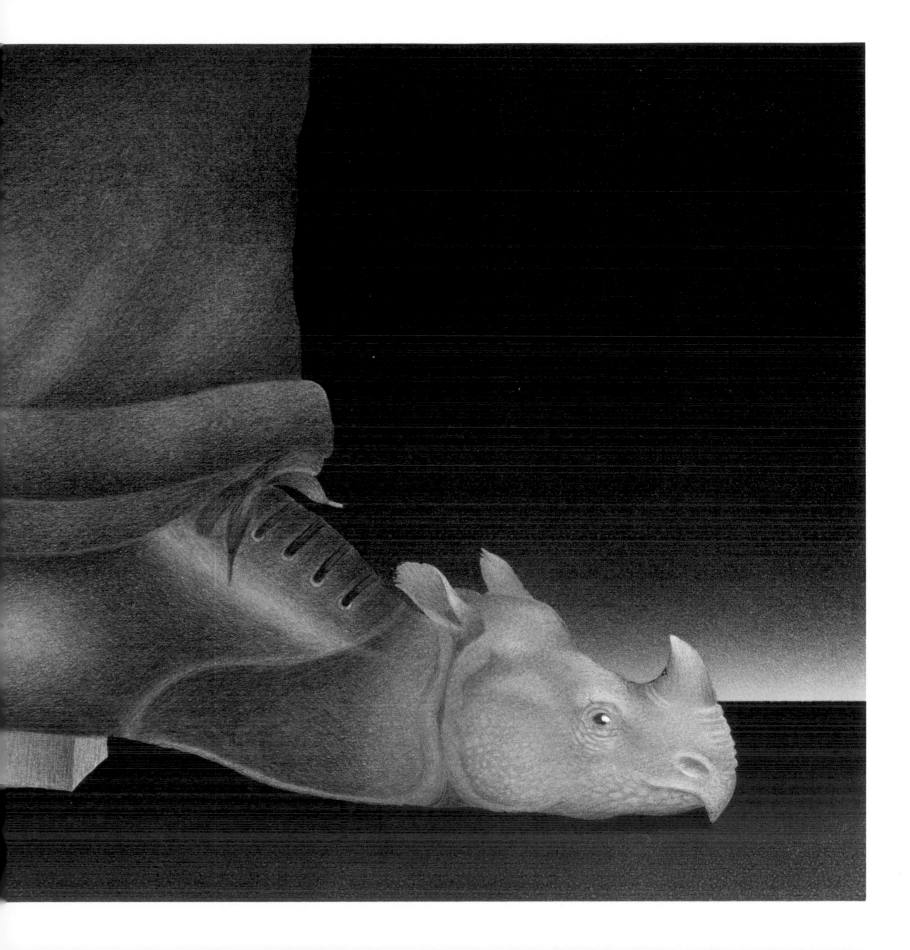

Mr. Milhous,
a rich man
who was rich for reasons still unknown,
thought at last
he was about to make contact
with Janice,
cow,
daughter of a steak,
future steak,
for an eventual communication.
But, for a reason still unknown,
he communicated
with Gladys,
an apple,
daughter of an apple core,
future apple core.

Shhh!
Moral :
Don't believe
everything
you read.
Or see.
Or hear.